What do you love about the carnival?

The rides, because they
are fast and wicked!
— Zhakya

I love the sticky pink
cotton candy!
— Libby

I like hot dogs that are as
big as your arm!
— Sienna

The spooooky haunted houses,
because they're super scary!
— Freya

I love the cotton candy
because it's so FLUFFY!
— Anna

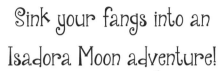

Sink your fangs into an
Isadora Moon adventure!

Isadora Moon Goes to School

Isadora Moon Goes Camping

Isadora Moon Goes to the Ballet

Isadora Moon Has a Birthday

Isadora Moon Goes on a Field Trip

Isadora Moon Saves the Carnival

Coming Soon!

Isadora Moon Has a Sleepover

ISADORA MOON

Saves the Carnival

Harriet Muncaster

A STEPPING STONE BOOK™

Random House 🏠 New York

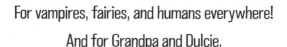

For vampires, fairies, and humans everywhere!
And for Grandpa and Dulcie.

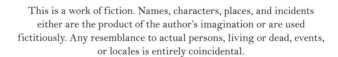

This is a work of fiction. Names, characters, places, and incidents either are the product of the author's imagination or are used fictitiously. Any resemblance to actual persons, living or dead, events, or locales is entirely coincidental.

Visit us on the Web!
rhcbooks.com

Educators and librarians, for a variety of teaching tools, visit us at RHTeachersLibrarians.com

Library of Congress Cataloging-in-Publication Data is available upon request.
ISBN 978-1-9848-5174-1 (pbk.) — ISBN 978-1-9848-5175-8 (ebook)

MANUFACTURED IN CHINA
10 9 8 7 6 5 4 3 2 1
First American Edition

This book has been officially leveled by using the
F&P Text Level Gradient™ Leveling System.

ISADORA MOON

Saves the Carnival

Chapter One

It was Saturday morning and the sun was shining through our windows. It made me feel all happy and sparkly and as though something interesting might happen.

"I wonder what it will be," I said to Pink Rabbit as we made our way down the stairs to breakfast.

Pink Rabbit bounced up and down beside me. He used to be my favorite stuffed toy, but my mom brought him to life with her wand. She can do things like that because she's a fairy!

"Good morning, Isadora," yawned Dad, who was just coming in through the front door. He had been on his nightly fly. Dad is a vampire, so he stays up all night and sleeps during the daytime. He stepped into the hallway, and I noticed that he was standing on a colorful piece of paper lying by the doormat.

"What's that?" I said, pulling it out from under his shiny black shoe.

"Junk mail probably," said Dad.

But it didn't look like junk mail to me. As I smoothed out the crumples, I saw that the piece of paper was a big glittering poster with a picture of a carousel in the middle of it. The carousel was covered with twinkle lights and spinning under a starry sky. Delighted children sat on top of fancily dressed ponies and held clouds of fluffy pink cotton candy in their hands. **CARNIVAL SPECTACULAR!** shouted the bold writing above the carousel. **NEXT WEEKEND ONLY!**

"Oh wow, Dad!" I said. "Can we go? Please?"

"Hmm," said Dad as I followed him into the kitchen. "I'm not sure. Ask Mom."

She was at the kitchen table with my baby sister. Mom was spooning strawberry yogurt into Honeyblossom's mouth. I held the poster up for Mom to see.

"Look!" I said. "Can we go?"

"A carnival?" said Mom dubiously. "A human fair . . . I'm not sure. Ask Dad."

"I've asked Dad!" I cried. "He told me to ask you!"

"Oh," said Mom, taking another look at the poster. "Well . . . "

"Please," I begged.

"Wouldn't you rather go to a vampire carnival?" asked Dad. "I used to love going to vampire carnivals with my friends when I was a young boy. All those spooky rides lit by flickering candles in the dead of night. And delicious red food. My favorite ride was the coffin blaster."

"Or we could go to a fairy carnival," suggested Mom quickly. "Fairy carnivals are lovely. All full of flowers and beautiful nature. I used to like going on the little flower-cup ride with my friends."

"Pfft!" said Dad. "The coffin blaster is much more exciting!"

"But not as pretty," pointed out Mom.

"Oh, but I really, really would like to go to the Carnival Spectacular," I said. "And it's only open next weekend. Please can we go? I promise I'll clean my whole bedroom!"

"Maybe," said Mom. "We'll think about it."

Chapter Two

When I went to school the following week, I asked my friends if they had seen that the Carnival Spectacular was coming to town.

"I saw a poster for the carnival on my way to school!" said Zoe. "I'm going to ask my mom if she'll take me!"

"I want to go too," said Bruno. "I'm going to ask my dad."

"So am I!" said Jasper.

My friends started talking excitedly about the carnival.

"I want to go on the roller coaster," said Sashi. "I've heard it has one hundred loops!"

"One hundred!" gasped Bruno. "I'm definitely going on that!"

"I'm not," said Samantha. She looked a little scared. "I prefer the teacups."

"Teacups are boring," said Jasper. "The bumper cars and the haunted-house ride are much more exciting!"

"Ooh yes, the haunted house!" said Zoe, shivering with glee. "And we can eat cotton candy and hot dogs."

"I love cotton candy!" cried Sashi. "It's like eating clouds!"

"Will you come, Isadora?" said Zoe, looking at me. "I bet you've never been to a human carnival before."

"I haven't," I said. "And I really want to go. I'll have to ask my mom and dad again."

All day I thought about how I would persuade them to let me go. By evening I had thought of a whole list of things I could do.

"Mom," I said. "If you take me to the carnival, I promise to water all your fairy plants for a whole week. And I'll help change

Honeyblossom's diapers every day. And give her pink milk. AND I'll even take all my baths in the garden pond from now on, to be close to nature."

Mom laughed. "That's very kind, Isadora," she said, "but—"

"And, Dad," I continued, "I promise to polish all of your special vampire silver. And hang my cape up by the front door so that it doesn't get creased. I'll clean my bedroom, and I *might* even brush my hair."

"Wow," said Dad, looking shocked. "You must really want to go to the carnival!"

"I do!" I said, thinking about the glittering carousel and the cotton candy and all the sparkling twinkle lights. I wanted to ride on one of the carousel ponies, with my hair flying in the breeze.

"Well," said Mom. "I was going to say that we had decided we would take you anyway. But as you've offered to do all these wonderful things for us . . ."

"It would be rude of us not to accept!" finished Dad. "My silverware is all laid out in the dining hall. I was thinking about polishing it this evening, but you can do it instead. There are only one hundred and ninety-nine pieces."

"And I think Honeyblossom does need a change," said Mom, sniffing the air. "You can do that too!"

I stared in horror at my baby sister, who was sitting, gurgling, in her high chair. I had never changed a diaper before.

"Um . . . ," I said, feeling my cheeks turn bright pink.

Mom and Dad both burst out laughing.

"It's all right, Isadora," said Mom. "We're
only joking."

"Though it would be nice if you cleaned
your room," said Dad.

"Yes, that would be lovely," agreed Mom.
Then suddenly she frowned and slapped
her hand to her forehead. "Wait!" she said.

"I forgot! Your cousins are coming next weekend! We can't go to the carnival. I'm sorry, Isadora. It completely slipped my mind."

"But couldn't we all go?" I suggested. "I bet Mirabelle and Wilbur would enjoy it."

"Well . . . I *suppose* we could ask them," said Mom. "And it would keep your cousin Mirabelle out of trouble, at least."

"Oh goody!" I said, hugging Pink Rabbit excitedly to my chest. "I can't wait!"

Chapter
Three

On the morning of the carnival I woke up
bright and early and jumped out of bed. I
was so excited.

"When will Mirabelle and Wilbur be
here?" I asked as I sat down at the kitchen
table. I began to eat my breakfast.

"Not until late afternoon," said Mom,

looking at the clock. "In about nine hours."

"Nine hours?!" I said. "That's ages!"

"I'm sure you'll find something to do," said Mom. "Why don't you clean your bedroom, like you promised?"

"Okaaay," I sighed.

It took me a long time to clean my room because it was so boring. The hours crept by very slowly. I watched the clock as it tick-tocked toward lunch and then tick-tocked into the afternoon.

"How long now?" I asked, staring out the kitchen window.

"About one hour," said Mom, who was busy making a strawberry cake. "You can help me decorate the cake if you like."

I stood by the table and sprinkled sugar bats and pink stars onto the swirly strawberry icing, but I kept one eye on the window. Eventually I saw a movement in the clouds outside.

"They're here!" I yelled, leaping toward the front door and opening it wide. Two figures were coming down through the clouds on broomsticks: my witch fairy cousin, Mirabelle, and her wizard fairy brother, Wilbur.

"Isadora!" shouted Mirabelle, landing on the ground and then running forward to hug me. She had obviously been spraying herself with her mom's witchy perfumes, because she smelled a lot like marzipan and purple berries.

"I'm so excited to go to the carnival!" she said. "Wilbur is too!"

"I guess so," said Wilbur, shrugging. He acted like he was too important to go to the carnival.

"We've never been to a human one before," said Mirabelle. "Mom's taken us to a witch one, though. It was really fun. There was an amazing broomstick ride and a fortune-telling tent and a black-cauldron Tilt-A-Whirl."

"There was," nodded Wilbur, starting to look a bit more excited. "I liked the wizard-hat spiral best.

It was a giant pointy wizard's hat with a slide twirling all the way down."

"I hope there'll be some fun rides at this carnival," continued Mirabelle. "I like the fast ones."

We all went inside and had some milk and cake while we waited for Dad to wake up. Being a vampire, he sleeps through the day and wakes up in the evening. I got the poster of the Carnival Spectacular from my bedroom and showed it to Mirabelle and Wilbur.

"It does look exciting," said Wilbur. "Though it is missing the wizard-hat spiral."

"It still looks very pretty and magical, though," said Mirabelle.

"It looks almost like the fairy carnivals I used to go to as a child," said my mom. "Your dad and I used to have so much fun at them together. Has your dad ever taken you to one?"

Wilbur and Mirabelle shook their heads.

"Ahh," said Mom. "Get him to take you one day. They are so exciting." She started to tell us about all the wonderful things that went on at fairy carnivals: the teacup flowers, the cones of sugared-violet candies, the little leaf boats in the boating pond. She was still talking away when Dad came into the kitchen, yawning and stretching.

"Good evening," he said. "Hello, Mirabelle. Hello, Wilbur!"

"Hello, Uncle Bartholomew," they said.

Once we had finished our milk, and Dad had drunk his red juice, we put on our shoes and got ready to go out to the carnival. It was a warm evening, and my insides fizzled with excitement as we headed toward town. As we walked, I reminded everyone that this was a human carnival.

"There won't be any magic," I said.

27

"And we can't do magic there either."

"Absolutely," said Mirabelle.

"Of course!" said Mom, waving her wand in the air. "I understand!" Little stars sparkled in the sky for a minute and then

disappeared. Mom stared at them happily.

"So pretty!" she breathed.

I pointed at the wand.

"That's the kind of thing I mean," I said.
"You need to hide that in your bag."

"Oh," said Mom. "Yes, of course." She quickly stowed the wand away in her handbag.

"Good!" I said, running ahead of everyone and rounding the corner. I wanted to be the first to see the carnival! I had visions of twinkling lights and striped tents and beautiful, colorful, sparkling rides. . . .

But what I actually saw made me stop in my tracks.

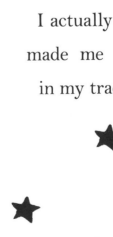

"Is this it?" asked Wilbur, sounding disappointed.

"It looks a bit run-down to me," said Dad, pursing his lips.

"It's not very busy, is it?" said Mom.

CARNIVAL
SPECTACULAR

BUMPER CARS

Chapter Four

The Carnival Spectacular did not look very spectacular at all. In fact, it looked very *un*spectacular. The striped tents were gray and tattered. The rides clanked and rattled. The music was so quiet you could barely hear it. And the twinkle lights were fizzing and spluttering as though they were about to go

out. The people operating the rides looked
sad and gray too. They had worry lines all
over their faces.

"Oh no . . . ," said Mom sadly. "What a
shame."

My heart suddenly felt very small and
tight. I held on to Mom's hand for a minute
because my eyes were stinging. I wasn't sure

if I wanted to visit a human carnival after all. Perhaps I should have listened to Mom and Dad and gone to a vampire or fairy one. I was embarrassed to have brought my whole family here.

"Maybe we should go home," I suggested.

"Nonsense!" said Mom, who always liked to look on the bright side. "We just got here! It's not that bad, Isadora. The rides are only a little run-down. Nothing some magic can't fix."

"Ooh yes!" said Mirabelle, rubbing her hands together gleefully. "I bet we could make this human carnival a whole lot more exciting!"

"No!" I cried. "No magic, remember?"

"Okay," said Mom, sounding slightly disappointed. "Well, let's go in anyway. I want to ride the teacups."

"The teacups!" scoffed Mirabelle. "I think we should go on the roller coaster! Or the haunted-house ride!"

CARNIVAL SPECTACULAR

I didn't feel like going on any of the rides, but I followed my family into the carnival and toward the roller coaster. As we got closer I could see that the paint was faded and peeling.

"At least we won't have to wait in line!" said Dad cheerfully as we walked up to the man in the ticket booth.

"Five tickets, please," Dad said.

The man in the booth lit up.

"Five!" he exclaimed. "Excellent! That's the most tickets we've sold so far tonight!"

"Why?" asked Dad. "Aren't you getting many customers?"

"Not as many as we used to," admitted the man.

"What a shame," said Mom.

"It is," agreed the man. "The problem is that a lot of our rides need updating. But we can't afford to fix them because we don't get enough customers. And the customers won't come because the rides need work. You can see the pickle we're in."

"I can," said Dad, nodding. "It's a conundrum."

"A conundrum?" said the man, scratching his head.

"It's a fancy word for a pickle," Dad explained.

"Ah," said the man. "Yes, it really is a conundrum. I hope we'll be able to think of a solution soon, or we might have to close the carnival down. It would be such a shame. It's a family-run business, you know. Started by my great-grandfather. It's traveled all over the country, and it's been going for almost one hundred years!"

"Wow!" exclaimed Mom. "One hundred years!"

"Well, in that case," said Dad kindly, "we'll take two rides each!" He put some money down on the counter, and we all stepped into the roller coaster. It was my first roller-coaster ride, and I was nervous. Pink Rabbit was nevous too—he had his paws over his eyes. A little bell rang, and

suddenly the roller coaster lurched to life. It
went clanking and clunking up the track and
then stopped at the top.

"Hang on!" called the man from below. "It's

stuck!" We saw him pushing some buttons, and then suddenly the car whooshed over the top of the track and swooped downward. It looped the loop and then came to another standstill in the middle of the track.

"Well, this is no good!" said Dad.

"It's not great," agreed Mirabelle.

"It's perfectly fast enough for me!" said Mom, who had her eyes tightly shut.

"Hmm," said Mirabelle. "I think this ride could use just a little help." Before I was able to stop her, she whipped out a small potion bottle and sploshed the contents onto the roller-coaster track. Immediately, the peeling paint began to repair itself. The run-down roller coaster became new and shiny once again. The clanking and clunking stopped, and suddenly we were gliding smoothly along the track at super-high speed. My hair blew out behind me and my tummy felt like it was turning upside down.

"Woo-hoo!" shrieked Mirabelle. "This is much more fun!"

After it had been around the track twice, the roller coaster came to a stop, and we all tumbled out on wobbly legs.

"I don't know what happened!" the ticket booth operator was saying to another carnival worker. "The ride just suddenly transformed! Look at it. Good as new!"

I frowned at Mirabelle and reminded her that this was a human carnival.

"We really shouldn't be using any magic," I said.

"I know, I know!" said Mirabelle. "But a little bit won't matter."

"Yes," agreed Mom. "A tiny bit won't make much of a difference. I mean, honestly, that roller coaster was a health-and-safety hazard!"

"It was a bit," agreed Dad. "And look how pleased the ticket man is!"

I saw the man beaming. He looked like he might burst with happiness.

"Maybe we *should* do a little fixing here

and there," whispered Mom. "You know, just to help the carnival."

"I think so," said Dad.

"Me too!" said Mirabelle excitedly.

"And me!" said Wilbur.

"Umm . . . ," I began. I wasn't sure if it was a good idea. Humans are not used to magic. I thought it might scare the customers away rather than bring them in.

"I vote for the teacups next," said Mom. "It's such a sophisticated ride."

"Boring, more like," whispered Wilbur as we made our way over to them.

Chapter Five

Dad bought our tickets, and we split ourselves among four of the teacups. The fifth one was broken, with a huge crack in one side of it. The ride started and we began to spin around slowly. The ride made a horrible creaking sound.

"Relaxing," said Mom.

"Booooring!" yawned Wilbur. I saw him wave his hands in a wizardy sort of way. Little sparks erupted from his fingers.

"What are you doing?" I whispered.

"Just helping it along a bit," said Wilbur. Suddenly, we began to spin so fast that everything became a blur. I started to feel sick.

"Wilbur!" shouted Dad. "Undo that spell this instant!!"

"This isn't what we meant by fixing the rides!" said Mom as her flower crown blew off her head.

Through the blur, I saw Wilbur's hands working to try to undo the spell he had cast. Eventually, the teacups slowed down. The

creaking sound came back. When I didn't feel so dizzy anymore, I could see the ride operator standing there with his mouth open. He was blinking his eyes and shaking his head in confusion.

"Let me do it," said Mom. She took out her wand and gave it a little wave so that glitter fell all around us. At once, the creaking sound stopped and we began to spin around as though everything was perfectly oiled. The crack in the broken teacup mended itself instantly.

"That's better," she said. "I might just add one more little improvement."

"No!" I cried. "We've done enough!"

But Mom had already waved her wand,

and suddenly, instead of teacups, we were sitting in giant, living, perfumed flowers that spun around gently and played beautiful music.

"Much more nature friendly." Mom smiled happily.

The new "teacups" were pretty, and the

ride operator looked delighted. Still, I was nervous about using magic at a human carnival.

"Stop worrying, Isadora!" said Wilbur. "Just relax!"

But I noticed that his nose had turned very red.

"Achoo!" he sneezed. "ACHOO!"

"Oh, help!" Dad shrieked, suddenly leaping out of his flower. "Bees are coming!" He covered himself in his cape and crouched down on the ground.

"Bees won't harm you!" sang Mom as she watched more and more of them buzz toward the flowers. "They're a very important part of nature!"

But Mirabelle, Wilbur, and I jumped out of our flower cups too. We stood on the grass, away from the big flowers and the bees.

"Achoo," sneezed Wilbur again. "I think that ride has set off my hay fever."

"Mom!" I called. "You need to undo your spell!"

54

"But why?" said Mom. "The flowers are so beautiful! Look at them!"

"The bees," whimpered Dad from under his cape. "The bees . . ."

Mom rolled her eyes and waved her wand. The flower cups turned back into ordinary teacups, but now they looked fresh and brand-new. I breathed a sigh of relief, and Dad cautiously looked out from under his cape.

"Can we stop doing magic now?" I asked as we all walked away from the ride.

"Yes, of course," said Dad. "Ooh, look, the bumper cars!"

"My favorite!" said Wilbur.

"Mine too!" said Mirabelle, grabbing a rusty car and hopping into it. She began to race around, shrieking with laughter every time she managed to bash into Wilbur.

"Hey, Mirabelle!" shouted Wilbur. "Calm down!"

"Yes, be careful!" said Dad. He was slowly driving around the floor, making sure to avoid bumping into anything.

"This is fun!" said Mirabelle as she zoomed her car toward Wilbur and bumped into

him. His wizard's hat fell over his eyes.

"So fun!" said Wilbur, doing a U-turn and bumping right back into her. "Got you, Mirabelle!"

"Got you both!" laughed Mom, who was sitting next to me and holding the wheel. She whizzed past them, crashing into both of their cars. Then she made a beeline for Dad, who was gliding about elegantly, avoiding everyone so that no one bashed into him and messed up his hair. She gave a little bump to the back of his car.

"What fun!" she whooped.

"You know what would make it more fun?" said Dad as he smoothed his hair back down. "These bumper cars would be much better if they had bat wings and could fly."

"Oh, no!" I said. "You said no more magic. Let's leave them as they are!"

"But bat wings would be amazing!" said Dad. "Vampire-bat cars! Oh, come on, just one more little spell!"

"Let's do it!" shouted Mirabelle as she screeched past us. I saw her let go of the wheel and get out her potion kit once again. She mixed something up at lightning speed and threw it into the air. The bumper cars transformed into sleek, black, bat-winged cars and began to rise upward.

59

"Wheeee!" shouted Mirabelle as she sailed around after Wilbur. "I'm coming to get you!"

"Not if I get you first!" shouted Wilbur.

By the time we had finished our ride on the bumper cars, a little crowd had gathered by the edge. Not just carnival workers but passersby too. They were all staring at the bumper cars in amazement. I spotted some of my friends from school in the crowd and waved.

"I want to go on these!" I overheard Bruno say.

"See," said Mom, patting my arm as we walked by. "A little bit of magic is not a bad thing. Look how many customers are starting to come!"

"I guess," I said, a little less worried. "Can we get some cotton candy now?"

Chapter Six

We made our way to the food stall, which smelled like hot dogs and burnt sugar. Mom got each of us our own cotton candy. It tasted like clouds!

"Yum," I said, biting into the fluff. It immediately melted on my tongue.

"You know what would make this cotton candy really exciting?" said Mom, waving her wand before anyone could say anything. "If it changed flavor with every bite!"

Sparkles rained down on us, and the next time I bit into my cotton candy, I tasted cherry pie.

"Ooh, butterscotch!" said Mirabelle.

"Chocolate cake!" said Wilbur.

"Frog legs," said Dad, wrinkling his nose.

"Oh," said Mom, "hang on." She waved her wand again.

"Red juice!" said Dad. "My favorite!"

I stared up at the sky, which was beginning to darken, and at the twinkle lights that were fizzing and spluttering all over the fairground. Some of the bulbs were

broken. After all the magic we had already done, fixing the twinkle lights wouldn't make much of a difference. Why shouldn't I help out a little bit too?

"Can I try to fix the lights?" I asked.

"Good idea," said Dad.

I closed my eyes tight and waved my wand above me, shooting a shower of sparks into the air. The broken lights began to twinkle and glow, and the fizzing and spluttering stopped.

"Beautiful, Isadora," said Mom.

Then I had another irresistible idea.

I waved my wand again, and this time the lights changed shape. Now they were all shaped like stars and moons and bats.

"Ooh, pretty!" said Mirabelle.

I felt my face glow pink with pride.

"I think we should go on that spinny thing next," said Wilbur, pointing toward a fast-looking ride that resembled a spider. There was a car at the end of each arm and the ride whizzed around and around.

"Umm . . . Pink Rabbit doesn't want to try that ride, so I'm going to stay here with him," I said.

"Me too," said Mom.

We walked over to the ride and looked on as Mirabelle, Wilbur, and Dad got into the little cars. The ride started, and we watched them rise up into the air and start to spin. Around and around they went, with their hair flying behind them. Suddenly, we saw a puff of magic powder explode out of Mirabelle's car, and all at once the ride transformed itself. My family were now sitting astride broomsticks instead of cars, and spinning higher and higher in the air. They weren't even attached to anything. I heard Mirabelle screech with delight, and the music from the ride started to blare across the fairground.

"Oh," said Mom. "I should have guessed she would do something!"

By the time the ride stopped, an even bigger crowd of people had gathered around.

"Wow!" they were saying. "We want a turn!"

The ticket seller was looking surprised but very pleased as he started to sell tickets to the next group of customers. Suddenly, I

didn't mind about the magic at all anymore, even though it meant that the carnival was not really a typical human one. It made me feel so happy that we had been able to help. My whole body tingled with excitement and pride. I wanted to do more! I pointed my wand at the roller coaster and shot a stream of sparks toward it. Fireworks began to shoot out of the back of the car as it sped along. Rainbow glitter and sparkles fizzed through the air.

"That's a nice touch, Isadora," said Mom. "I think we're really making a difference!"

"We are!" I said, feeling pleased.

"Where next?" asked Wilbur.

"The carousel!" I yelled.

"Good idea," said Dad. "We had better get there before the line gets too long!"

"I don't think there's much chance of there being a line," said Mom as we made our way over to the carousel, which sat in the middle of the fairground.

Sad and worn-looking horses bobbed up and down on poles as the carousel went

slowly around and around, playing a tune that kept getting stuck, so the same notes repeated again and again.

"Oh dear," said Dad. "This ride could use some help."

Chapter Seven

"I'll do it! I'll fix the carousel," I said, jumping up and down excitedly. "Let me try!"

I closed my eyes and waved my wand. When I opened them, the carousel horses had transformed into big, sparkling unicorns and glittering dragons with scaly wings. The music became jaunty and cheerful.

"Oh wow!" said my mom. "Well done, Isadora!"

"Beautiful!" said Dad.

We all raced toward the carousel. I chose a pink unicorn with a flowing mane and tail and hopped on. Pink Rabbit sat proudly in front of me.

We started to go around and around. But something magical was happening. The animals were starting to move. My unicorn began to stamp its feet, and suddenly, with the pole still attached, it leapt right off the carousel and began to bob around the fairground.

Mom, Dad, Mirabelle, and Wilbur followed right behind me on their animals.

We soared in and out of all the attractions. We went leaping through the air, with tiny glowing stars streaming out behind us. People stared as we flew by. They reached for their phones, took photos, and called their friends.

"Come to the carnival!" they shouted.

"You won't believe your eyes!"

Eventually, the animals went back toward the carousel and hopped on, waiting for the next group of people.

"That was amazing," said Mirabelle.

"It was my favorite!" I said.

There was a huge line waiting to get on

the carousel now, and the fairground was absolutely packed with people. I could see my friend Zoe climbing onto the pink unicorn. I waved to her, and she waved back.

"I think we've done enough," said Mom. "We should probably stop doing magic now."

"Yes," agreed Dad. "We don't want to

overdo it. Let's just enjoy ourselves. How about the haunted house?"

"I love haunted houses," said Mirabelle.

We lined up for the ride and waited for our turn. I noticed a glint in Mirabelle's eye. Once we were on the ride, she started to look in her pocket for something.

"What are you doing?" I asked. The train lurched to life and started to run along the track, passing pretend monsters that popped out of the shadows.

"Just one more thing," said Mirabelle. "The last time, I promise."

I saw her mix something up, and she threw it onto the monsters as we passed.

"It will just make the ride a little more interesting," she explained.

But "interesting" was not the word I would have used. When the train came out of the ride at the end, I could see people screaming and running away.

They looked *terrified.* Then I saw what Mirabelle had done. The monsters, which had been pretend before, had come to life! They were leaping out of the haunted-house ride and spilling out into the fairground, chasing after the crowds!

Chapter Eight

"Run!" screamed the people. "Monsters!"

"Oh, Mirabelle!" wailed Dad, putting his head in his hands. "What have you done?"

"Only the same as Isadora did to the carousel," said Mirabelle defensively, but I noticed that she didn't seem quite so sure of herself now.

"Well, you've gone too far!" said Dad. "Look at the people running away. All the good work we have done is ruined!"

We watched as the monsters caused trouble around the carnival. They didn't seem dangerous to me, just excitable and curious. They had lost interest in the people and had spotted the bright lights of the food stall. They began to hungrily gobble down hot dogs, popcorn, doughnuts, and rainbow cotton candy.

"Stop!" the owner of the food stall shouted. "Help!" He looked dismayed.

"We have to stop them," said Wilbur. "We need to think of something!"

"I have an idea," said Mom. She waved her wand, and a leafy vine streamed out of it. She tied it into a lasso. Then she made four more.

"Take these," she said, thrusting one out to each of us. "Let's try to round up the monsters!"

We each grabbed a lasso and ran through the carnival. It was chaos. People were running all over the place and screaming. Popcorn and hot dogs were flying through the air. I ran to the food stall and threw my lasso, but the monsters saw me coming. They laughed, thinking it was a great game, and started to run away, scattering across the fairground and starting to climb up the rides.

"Oh no!" cried Mom. "I think we need a better plan."

I flapped my little bat wings and rose into the air. I tried to lasso a monster that was crawling up the side of the roller coaster, but it was too strong for me. Instead, I was whooshed through the air as the monster took hold of my vine and started pulling me toward it. I needed something to fly on, something strong.

"The carousel!" I shouted, tugging the lasso away from the monster and flying over to my favorite ride. I landed on the back of a Pegasus and tugged gently on the reins. The magical creature leapt off the carousel and started to rise into the air, flapping its big, beautiful wings. Its body felt strong and solid beneath me. Out of the corner of my eye, I saw Wilbur jumping onto a dragon's back.

As we soared through the air, I spotted Dad shooting toward the hall of mirrors in a black bat-winged bumper car. Mirabelle

had hopped onto one of the broomsticks. We circled in the air above the carnival. People below stared up, open-mouthed.

I swirled my lasso in the sky and brought it down gently around one of the monsters that had jumped onto the roof of the carousel. The monster squeaked and looked surprised.

Mirabelle whirled her lasso and brought it down over a monster hiding behind the cotton-candy stall. Wilbur caught two monsters that were busy climbing

up the side of the roller coaster. It didn't take long to round them all up, and soon they were gathered in a little group in the middle of the fairground. Mom and Dad came running out of the hall of mirrors with one more monster, caught in the loops of their leafy vines.

"Well, that was fun," I heard Dad say. "More mirrors than you can imagine!"

"It wasn't the best time to stop and do your hair, though, was it?" said Mom, sounding slightly annoyed.

The monsters didn't look very scary at all—in fact, they looked a little frightened. I felt sorry for them.

"They won't hurt you!" I said to the crowd. "They were just playing."

"Though it was very naughty of you to eat all the food without paying," said Dad, staring sternly at the monsters. "You could make up for it by helping out!"

The monsters seemed excited by this idea.

"You could help sell the tickets and popcorn," I suggested. "Look at all the crowds of people. The carnival workers could probably use some extra help."

"We could!" agreed one of the ticket sellers. "That would be wonderful!"

Chapter Nine

The monsters seemed pleased to be helping. Enthusiastically, they bounded over to the different rides to help sell tickets. Some of them started picking up litter and putting it in bags. Others went back to the haunted-house ride to add some extra excitement.

"This is great!" said the carnival owner.

"You've really saved the day by rounding up all those monsters. We were worried we were going to lose all our new customers!"

"I don't think you're in danger of that now!" said Mom, looking around.

The carnival was bursting with people. There were lines snaking away from every ride. Children were screaming and laughing with glee. The twinkle lights were flashing, the music was blaring, and suddenly I realized that the carnival looked much more like the picture on the poster. I felt a glow of happiness flood through my whole body.

"You've really helped us out," continued the man. "We are so grateful."

"Oh, it was nothing!" said Dad, waving his hand dismissively in the air.

"It was our pleasure." Mom smiled. "Though you do realize that most of this magic is temporary? The carousel animals and the monsters won't stay alive forever."

"No worries!" said the man. "We'll have made enough money tonight to do all the repairs we need to our rides, and more! The Carnival Spectacular will be spectacular once again!"

"Excellent!" said Dad.

"I'm so glad," said Mom.

"We'd like to thank you all properly," said the man, "so please feel free to pick a prize of your choosing to take home." He gestured toward a stall where there were lots of big cuddly toys.

"Ooh, good," said Dad, bounding over

immediately and starting to examine the toys. I followed him and pointed to a big fluffy monster.

"May I have that one, please?" I asked.

"Of course!" said the carnival owner, unhooking it for me. Pink Rabbit bounced up and down beside me. I could tell he was getting jealous.

"Here's one for Pink Rabbit," said Mom, handing him a tiny stuffed-monster key ring. It was the perfect size for him, and Pink Rabbit wiggled his ears in delight.

Just then I noticed Zoe skip through the crowd toward me, with her mom in tow.

"Isadora!" she cried. "Have you seen the carousel? It has unicorns on it!"

"I have!" I said. "It's my favorite ride! Do
you want to go on it together?"

"I would love that!" said Zoe. She took

my hand, and we made our way back into the crowd, Pink Rabbit hopping along beside me, and my family following close behind.

There was a long line for the carousel, but it didn't matter. We ate hot dogs and rainbow cotton candy while we waited, and then Zoe and I hopped onto a unicorn together. Mirabelle and Wilbur chose a dragon, bickering over who was going to sit at the front, and Mom and Dad sat on a Pegasus pony with wings.

The music started, and we began to move. Around and around we went, our hair streaming behind us in the breeze, and twinkle lights flashing in our eyes. It didn't matter if we were at a human carnival or a magical carnival. I was just so happy to be there with my family and my friends, spinning and twirling under the starry sky. Just like the kids on the poster for the Carnival Spectacular.

Vampire-Fairy Cakes!

You will need an assistant, so make
sure an adult helps you.

⭐ Preheat the oven to 350°F.
Place cupcake liners in a 12-cup muffin pan.

  ⭐ In a large mixing bowl, combine 2/3 cup
margarine or butter with 3/4 cup sugar.

 ⭐ Mix in 3 eggs and 1 teaspoon
vanilla extract.

  ⭐ Sift in 1 1/2 cups all-purpose flour
and 1 teaspoon baking powder.

 ⭐ Mix until all ingredients are combined.
Then spoon a tablespoon of the mixture
into each of the muffin cups.

 ⭐ In each cup, make a well in the batter with a
teaspoon or clean finger. Fill it with a teaspoon
of strawberry jam.

★ Fill the cups with cake mixture until they are 3/4 full. Then bake the cakes for 8–10 minutes. When they are golden brown, remove them from the oven and let them cool on a wire rack.

★ Once the cakes are cool, spread the top with a blob of strawberry jam. You can make fangs out of white fondant or icing, use gummy candies, or even top with wearable plastic fangs.

Which character are you?

Take the quiz to find out!

What's your favorite ride at the carnival?

A. a roller coaster with lots of loops!

B. the carousel—my favorite is the unicorn

C. the spiral slide

What's your favorite food to eat at the carnival?

A. a big bag of candy

B. cotton candy

C. a hot dog

If you could do some magic at the carnival, what would you do?

A. I would make all the rides super fast.

B. I would transform the whole carnival to make everything there totally magical!

C. I would conjure up a wizard-hat spiral slide.

Mostly As

You are Mirabelle! You have a mischievous sense of
fun, and you are a great friend to have around!

Mostly Bs

You are Isadora! You have an amazing imagination,
and you are a really generous friend.

Mostly Cs

You are Wilbur! You are talented and smart,
and you love to have fun.

RESULTS

Family Tree

My mom,
Countess Cordelia
Moon

Baby Honeyblossom

My dad,
Count Bartholomew
Moon

Me!
Isadora Moon

Pink Rabbit

Sink your fangs into another
Isadora Moon adventure!

Has a Sleepover

I love Zoe's bedroom. It is always so interesting. There are butterflies painted on her walls, and loads of posters stuck on her closet door. She also has the biggest dress-up box of everyone I know.

"Want to play dress-up?" I said, opening up the box and beginning to rummage inside.

"Sure!" said Zoe, taking out some pink fairy wings and a sparkly silver crown. She put them on, then added a pair of slip-on shoes with pom-poms on the toes.

"I know," she said. "Why don't I be a fairy queen, and you be a vampire queen? We can be best friends, but the rulers of different kingdoms. My kingdom will be on a fluffy pink cloud! I'm going to have a palace there made from glass, and everything will smell of roses." She began to spray herself all over with a flower-scented perfume.

"Okay," I said, taking a tall shimmery black crown from the box and putting it on my head. "My kingdom will be up in the night sky, surrounded by glittering stars, and I will have one hundred pet bats. And Pink Rabbit will be a vampire prince!"

Pink Rabbit looked pleased at my

suggestion and began to hop up and down happily.

"Coco will be a fairy princess!" said Zoe, picking up her favorite toy monkey from her pillow and hugging it to her chest. Pink Rabbit watched interestedly. Then he bounced over to Zoe and held out his paw.

"Pink Rabbit wants to shake Coco's hand," I said.

Zoe knelt down and held her monkey out to Pink Rabbit.

"Coco is pleased to meet you," she said, and Pink Rabbit's ears twitched with happiness. He began to stroke Coco's stripy tail.

"I think they like each other," I said.

"I think so too!" laughed Zoe. Then a wistful look came over her face.

"Isadora," she said, "do you think that maybe . . . maybe you could magic Coco alive, just for our game? I think Pink Rabbit would love it. And I would too!"

I glanced over at my wand, poking out from my bag in the corner of the room.

"I guess I could," I replied, hurrying over to fetch the wand.

Zoe started to jump up and down with excitement.

"Could you?" she whispered. "Really?"

"I'll try," I said. "I've only done this spell once before, though. It might take me a few tries." I pointed my wand at Coco the monkey and squeezed my eyes tightly shut. I waved my wand,

then opened my eyes. A stream of
twinkly sparks floated down onto
Coco, landing all over her fur.

"Ooh!" sighed Zoe in wonder.

The sparks began to fade, and
underneath them, Coco blinked her
button eyes. The spell had worked on
the first try!

New friends. Ne[...]
Find a new series [...]

ISADORA MOON

Isadora Moon Goes to School

Harriet Muncaster

For ballerina and fairy and vampire lovers

COMMANDER IN CHEESE

Commander in Cheese: The Big Move

Lindsey Leavitt, illustrated by A. G. Ford

For adventurers

JULIAN'S WORLD: THE STORIES JULIAN TELLS

Ann Cameron

For storytellers

PUPPY PIRATES

Puppy Pirates: Stowaway!

Erin Soderberg

For dog lovers

PuRRmaids

PuRRmaids: The Scaredy Cat

For mermaid and cat

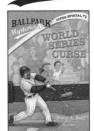

BALLPARK Mysteries

Ballpark Mysteries Super Special #1: THE WORLD SERIES CURSE

David A. Kelly

For sports

31901065097471

RHCB **RHCBooks.com**